The Tradition of the Fairy Door

Children around the world have noticed an
itty, bitty door somewhere in their room or house.
Some believe this is a tooth fairy door to allow her
to sneak in and gather her treasures. Some fairy
doors magically appear; the fairy knowing a
harvest is imminent. Some fairy doors are placed
there by children with the hope of enticing a fairy.
They may even decorate the inside of the door
(to the fairy world), so she will choose their room
to enter. However the door appears, it is magical!
Children should not be disappointed when they can
not open their fairy door, only the fairy has the key.
Do take the time to decorate the door and leave
little gifts!

Thank you for the memories, Ri, Little Man, Baba, Savvy, and Kahlo. Be brave with your lives.

Printed in the United States of America

March 2016

ISBN 978-0-692-64520-8

Kimberly Kilgore
Macoutah, IL

Behind
the *Fairy* Door

by Kimberly Wells Kilgore
illustrated by Tracey Taylor Arvidson

Behind this little door is a wonderful world to explore.

But only at night in your magical dreams with a little

help from fairy dust, and you it seems.

You see, behind this door is a land where dreams and memories grow.

Where rainbows shine forever,
and lightening bugs glow.

Where ninjas fight pirates in a foam sword dual.
Where kissing your mom will always be cool.

Where jumping on the bed is sometimes allowed,
and a good knock-knock joke makes you laugh out loud!

Where hide and seek is the best game in town,
and a stuffed animal tea party means you dress
up in a tiara and gown.

How do you get here, you must wonder, I suppose?
Well listen closely, here it goes!

It all starts with a wiggle, wiggle!

And a little jiggle, jiggle!

And for the impatient sort,
a door, a string, and a little tooth fling!

Then in your hand, you have what appears to be a tooth;

but to a fairy it is a treasure that will grow just like you!

Before you tuck into bed,
you will place this treasure just under your head.

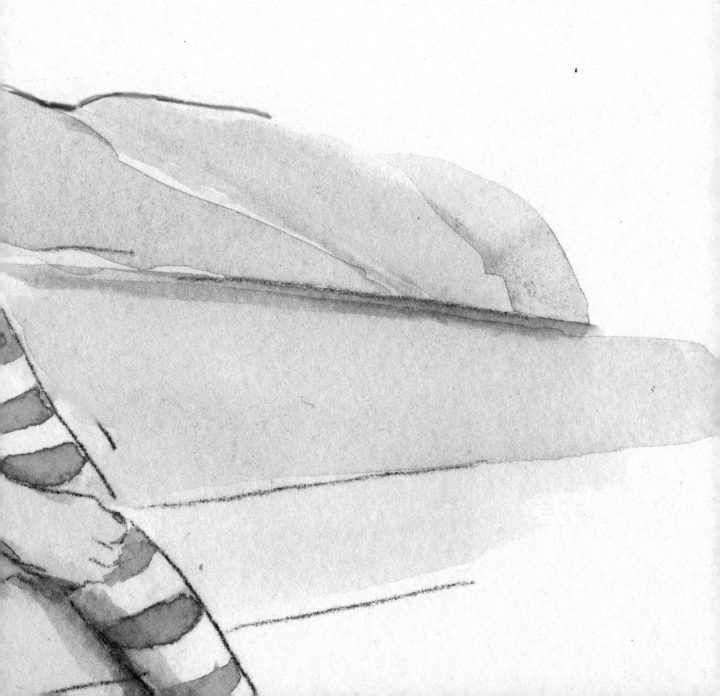

While you are sleeping and sweet
dreams are abound,

your Fairy will travel through the little door
without a sound.

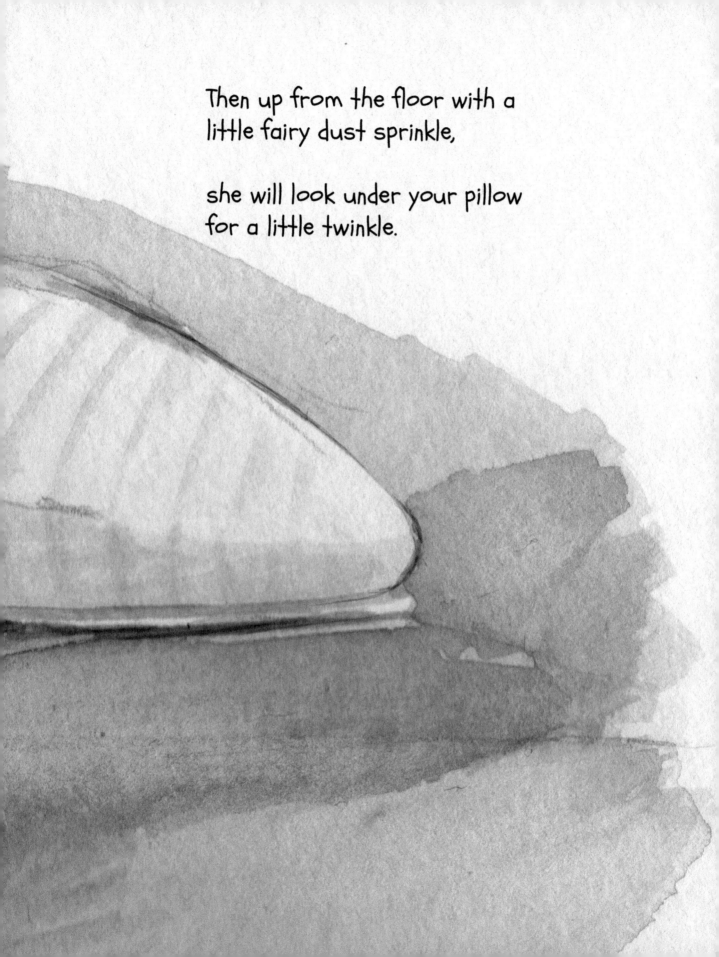

Then up from the floor with a
little fairy dust sprinkle,

she will look under your pillow
for a little twinkle.

But wait, there is more!
You see, she checks to see if your room is nice and neat.

She looks at your homework to make sure it's complete.

5 + 4 = 9
4 + 5 = 9
8 + 1 = 9
1 + 8 = 9
3 + 6 = 9
6 + 3 = 9

3 + 6

And if the tooth is nice and clean,

she leaves you a treasure,

something shiny or green.

Quickly back through the door she must go with treasure in hand.

She is off to plant this treasure in her little land.

Up will grow a flower fit for a queen,
and from it will come fairy dust and all the
magic it can bring.

A piece of you will always be in this magical place;
cherished so dearly, not even time will erase.

And every once in a while,
your fairy will come back
to visit at night.

She will sprinkle a little fairy
dust on your pillow
to help you sleep tight.

Oh! What a sparkly sight!

A sweet dream, a "remember when",
or lullaby is sure to follow!

It just must!
For that is the magic of fairy dust!

Your mom may even get a whiff when she tucks you in and gives you a kiss. She may start to sing that song she rocked you to sleep with long ago or talk, talk, talk about how you are growing so!

Hush little baby...

So keep your room clean
and your fairy door bright!

BUT MOST IMPORTANT OF ALL
BRUSH THOSE TEETH EVERY NIGHT!

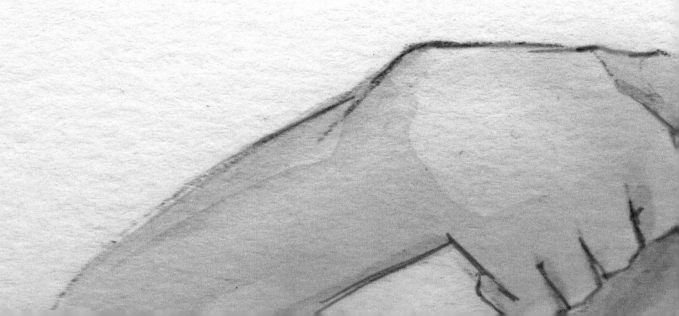

Sweet dreams little one, may your dreams be merry!
Thank you for the memories, your momma and your fairy.

CPSIA information can be obtained
at www.ICGtesting.com
Printed in the USA
LVOW05s0822190316

479876LV00006B/25/P